WELCOME TO SHANNA'S First Readers

Each **Level 1 Shanna First Reader** features:

- rhyme and rhythm
- picture clues
- easy words
- sight words
- phonics games
- large print

As children learn to read, they are most successful with books that feature rhyme and rhythm, repetition of words, predictable language, and decodable words. These elements are all "clues" that children use to sound out, read, and recognize new words. Below are some ways to utilize these "clues" with your child as you read **Shanna's Pizza Parlor**.

Repetition Clues For example, look for repeated words like *Come in! Come in!* If you read the first *Come in!* your child may be able to read the next one.

Rhythm and Rhyme Clues Children love rhythm and rhyme, and these features help them read. Anticipating a rhyme because of the rhythm helps children sound out words. The rhyme is a clue to the sound.

Phonics Clues If your child knows that the sound for the letter *M* can be "mmm" and that the sound for the letter *Y* can be "eye," then your child may be able to link the two sounds together and read *my*. You can help your child sound out words this way. But a word of caution: don't overdo it. Catching on to phonics is developmental. It happens when it happens—like walking and talking. Your job is to coach cheerfully and patiently. One appropriate phonics reading game you can play is to look for words that are similar. For example, you might ask, "How do the words *ham* and *jam* look and sound alike?"

Story Clues Help your child with words like *nutritious* and *delicious*. Kids like big words, and once they hear them, they'll remember them, even if they can't read them.

Picture Clues Point out the picture clues on Shanna's menu board in **Shanna's Pizza Parlor**. The pictures of the pizza toppings, along with their word labels, will help your child begin to recognize the words as they read the story.

Happy Reading!
Jean Marzollo

For Allen Thomas Edwards Martin

**Special thanks to Jackie Carter,
Editorial Director of Jump at the Sun,
for her commitment to helping children
learn to read enjoyably**

For information address Hyperion Books for Children,
114 Fifth Avenue, New York, New York 10011-5690.

Printed in the United States of America
First Edition
1 3 5 7 9 10 8 6 4 2

Library of Congress Cataloging-in-Publication Data on file.
ISBN 0-7868-1831-X

Visit www.jumpatthesun.com

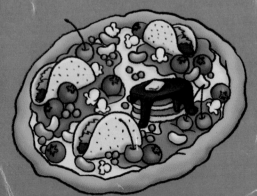

LEVEL 1 Shanna's FIRST READERS

Shanna's Pizza Parlor

By Jean Marzollo

Based on art by Shane W. Evans
Illustrated by Maryn Roos

Jump at the Sun/Hyperion Books for Children • New York

Come in. Come in.
Come in.
Come in to my pizza parlor.

Can I really have tomatoes and tacos on my pizza?

Okay!

Can I really have peas,
popcorn, and pancakes
on my pizza?

Can I really have cheese and cherries on my pizza?

Sure!

Can I really have jam and jelly beans on my pizza?

My pizza has tomatoes and tacos.

So I choose tea.

My pizza has peas,
popcorn, and pancakes.

So I choose punch.

My pizza has
cheese and cherries.

So I choose chocolate milk.

My pizza has
jam and jelly beans.

So I choose juice.

Mmmmm . . .
This is the best tomato, taco, pea, popcorn, pancake, cheese, cherry, jam, and jelly bean pizza I have ever had!

Shanna's Pizza Menu

Oh, no! Shanna is away.

Do you remember which drink went with each pizza today?

Draw a line to match each pizza to its drink.

 Tacos and tomatoes	 Juice
 Peas, popcorn, and pancakes	 Chocolate milk
 Cheese and cherries	 Punch
 Jam and jelly beans	 Tea